Iris the Dragon Story

Iris the Dragon is a spokesperson for children's mental health issues. Her primary goal is to educate caregivers and children about the importance of prevention and early identification of mental health. Iris the Dragon's mission statement is:

To create tools to help children and caregivers understand that early detection, risk management and education can help alleviate, if not prevent, mental illness in children and reaffirm the message that mental illness in children exists, is increasing and needs to be better understood.

Iris the Dragon Book Series

Iris the Dragon Inc. is proud to present their children's illustrated book series. Each book addresses a different mental disorder to provide hope for children that suffer from these disorders and education to those that do not.

Iris the Dragon books have been vetted and endorsed by professionals in the mental health and education field to realistically portray each mental illness introduced in the series.

"Catch a Falling Star: A Tale from the Iris the Dragon Series" is the first book in the Iris the Dragon series. "Catch a Falling Star" presents its readers with a variety of symptoms that could be considered red flags in a child's emotional and social development. This book is intended as an introduction to the topic of mental health in addition to educating children about the importance of sharing their thoughts and worries with a caregiver.

"Lucky Horseshoes: A Tale from the Iris the Dragon Series" addresses the topic of ADHD in children. This book provides children with ADHD an opportunity to identify with their thoughts, feelings and actions through the young character in the book. For caregivers, "Lucky Horseshoes" has an informative epilogue about ADHD from Dr. Catharine Robertson, Staff Psychiatrist at the Children's Hospital of Eastern Ontario and Chair of the ADHD Network of Eastern Ontario. In addition, the book illustrates the role of an Individual Education Plan (IEP) in helping a child achieve their potential.

Ian Millar Endorsement

"Little Ben sees only the beauty of the person within.

Little Ben has only a positive and honest agenda.

Little Ben knows there is always hope and that dreams can be achieved.

I have long believed that the partnership of human and horse as a therapeutic solution is effective and powerful.

When we understand children's mental illness, we have taken the first critical step towards conquering that illness.

Gayle Grass, I am awed by your creation of Little Ben, all that he stands for and all that he achieves."

Ian D. Millar

Ian D. Millar CM LLD

Ian Millar (born January 6, 1947) is a Canadian show-jumping world champion. Born in Halifax, Nova Scotia, Ian Millar is the most successful show-jumper in Canadian history. He is an eight-time winner of the Canadian Show Jumping Championship and has captured six Spruce Meadows Derbys. With his horse, Big Ben (1976-1999), Millar won more than 40 Grand Prix titles worldwide and the World Cup Finals for two years in a row. He holds the North American record for Grand Prix and Derby wins. He was a member of every Canadian Olympic Equestrian Team and World Show Jumping championship team since 1972. In 1986, he was made a Member of the Order of Canada.

Ian Millar operates "Millar Brooke Farms" near the small town of Perth, Ontario.

Lucky Horseshoes
a tale from
The Iris the Dragon Series

Author
Gayle Grass

With Illustrations
By Linda Crockett

A children's book dealing with ADHD

Fall

Skippy sat on an old rocking chair on her porch watching the river flow by. School was over for the day and she liked to sit and dream about horses. All of a sudden out of the corner of her eye, Skippy noticed a strange ripple moving upstream.

She ran down to the riverbank and stood on a loose pile of rocks to have a better look. Suddenly, she slipped and before she knew it, she had fallen into the fast flowing water.

As she was trying to swim to shore, Skippy felt something large and bumpy, like an old log, under her. The log appeared to be carrying her through the water towards the river's edge. As she rose out of the water, she saw that the log had a head with very large ears.

"Who are you?" Skippy screamed, when she realized the log was alive.

"I'm Iris, a green swamp dragon. Don't be scared Skippy, I'm really very friendly."

"Where do you come from?" asked Skippy as she studied Iris.

"I live down the river under the old bridge. I have my cave there. I was on my way home and saw you in the water. It looked like you needed some help. Can I sit and rest with you for a moment?" Iris asked, climbing out of the water.

"Sure and thanks for helping me. That was a close call," Skippy laughed nervously.

Skippy noticed that Iris was quite small for a dragon. On her head she wore an old straw hat with leaves and flowers stuck in it and on her back she carried an old dilapidated knapsack. But what caught Skippy's attention was Iris's beautiful green and blue wings as she spread them wide to dry in the breeze.

"I was just sitting on my porch dreaming of owning my own horse," Skippy continued. "Then I saw you in the water and I slipped on the rocks and fell in. Mom will be really mad when I tell her that I fell in the river. She says I'm always doing things without thinking. You know, like saying something before realizing it could get me into trouble."

"Or like running to the edge of the water without thinking the rocks could be slippery?" prompted Iris.

"Right," smiled Skippy realizing Iris understood.

"Why do they call you Skippy?" Iris continued. "It is an unusual name."

"Yes," replied Skippy, "my dad gave me that nickname when I was little because he said that ever since I could walk, I have always been skipping here and skipping there. My Dad died when I was very young so I don't really remember him very well, but everyone still calls me Skippy."

Iris thought for a moment and then she said, "Skippy, I have an idea. Would you like to go on an excursion with me tomorrow to meet some of my riverbank friends?"

Skippy was so excited that she jumped up and down and exclaimed: "When can we go?"

"We will go tomorrow after school. Now please go home and get into some dry clothes," laughed Iris.

The next day at school, Skippy had her usual problems. She found it very hard to concentrate. The sounds in the halls, the shouts and laughing of the children in the yard, and even the lights in the classroom bothered her. She tried to avoid them by moving around in her chair but this got her into trouble. Often the best way to ignore the noises was to daydream.

As soon as the bell rang, Skippy dashed out of school as fast as she could and raced home. Rounding the corner of her house, her foot caught on the edge of the porch.

"Ouch," yelped Skippy, as she fell flat on her face.

"Are you OK?" cried Iris, hurrying out of the water.

"I think so, but my knee hurts," sniffed Skippy.

"Let me take a look at it. I know a lot about scrapes and bruises," said Iris. "The riverbank animals are always coming to me to treat their injuries."

Iris gently cleaned Skippy's knee. Then she reached into her knapsack and took out a little package.

"I never leave home without this cream. It is some healing cream that I made myself," Iris said as she spread some over Skippy's knee.

"That smells funny," said Skippy wrinkling her nose.

"It's made from the finest riverbank herbs and plants. It works wonders," explained Iris.

After spreading the cream, Iris reached into her knapsack again and pulled out a large red handkerchief. Wrapping it around Skippy's knee, she said:

"There, that will help it. Now climb on my back and hold on to my knapsack."

Iris and Skippy had a wonderful afternoon. Just down the river they met up with some of Iris's friends, Madeleine Frog and Ottie Otter. Madeleine was very shy but gradually showed Skippy her baby frogies. Ottie Otter was his usual chatty self and never stopped talking. He wanted to show off for Skippy so he kept sliding down the river bank and plunging into the river. Skippy loved meeting them and gave them each a little hand shake as they left.

On the way home, Skippy told Iris that this was one of the happiest days of her life. "You know Iris," she said, "right now I feel really relaxed. But sometimes I get so frustrated I get really angry and I think I'm going to explode. It mostly happens when I feel I can't do anything right. Then I scream at my mom and break things. I feel really bad afterwards as my mom tries so hard to help me."

Iris nodded her head. She understood that something was causing Skippy to feel like this and she knew that it would take a lot of time and patience to figure out exactly what Skippy's problem was. She also knew that there were people who could help Skippy and she was hopeful that together they could all help Skippy feel less angry and more confident about herself.

When they reached the shore in front of Skippy's house, Iris asked. "Would you like to take another trip this weekend? I would like you to meet a little colt called Little Ben. He is only a few months old."

Skippy's face lit up in a big smile and she danced around Iris.

"That would be the best. I have never seen a baby horse. I'll be waiting at the riverbank Iris. I can hardly wait," she yelled as she ran up the path to her house.

  Lucky Horseshoes

When Skippy woke up on Saturday, the sun was streaming through her window. "This is going to be a great day," she thought as she jumped out of bed.

But over breakfast, the problems started.

"Skippy, I want to talk to you about something," her mother began. "You know last year you had problems at school. No matter how hard you tried, you often couldn't sit still. And the teacher kept saying you weren't trying hard enough even though you thought you were? She said you weren't focused and were forgetting to do your homework?"

"I remember Mom and I'm really trying this year, but I still get into trouble," Skippy replied.

"I know, and last week I went and talked to your new teacher. She said the reason you might be getting angry at times may have something to do with the way your brain works. She thinks I should talk to the principal and ask that we get special tests for you. Then we can see what the problem really is and figure out ways to make it better."

"Aw Mom no," screamed Skippy, suddenly getting very angry. "I don't need these tests. It won't help. All the other kids will find out that I'm having them and they will laugh at me. They'll think I'm different."

Skippy was so upset that she ran out of the house, knocking her breakfast all over the floor. With tears in her eyes, Skippy ran down to the river and along the path that led to the wooden bridge and Iris's cave.

All of a sudden, she heard a strange noise. She stopped. It sounded like a horse's whinny. But what would a horse be doing here? She stepped forward very quietly, and just around the bend, behind some bushes, she saw a baby colt. His ears were back and he looked frightened. Skippy moved slowly forward. As the colt strained forward to get a sniff of her, his hoof slipped on a rock and he went down, banging his knee.

Just then, Iris appeared.

"Oh Iris, I think I frightened the little horse and he's hurt. Can you help him?" Skippy whispered.

Iris came towards the colt. She rubbed noses with him and whispered something in his ear.

"What did he say, what did he say?" Skippy asked impatiently. "Is he alright?"

"I'm just going to look at his knee. Be very quiet," Iris answered. She reached into her knapsack and took out her healing cream. With her red handkerchief, she carefully bandaged the colt's knee.

"Skippy come and meet Little Ben. He is fine but a little scared as he wandered too far away from his mother and got lost. I told him I will take him home."

Skippy walked slowly up to Little Ben so as not to scare him. When she got close she stood very still. Little Ben sniffed her gently and then put his head down and rubbed his nose against Skippy's arm.

"He likes you Skippy," said Iris.

"I like him too," said Skippy shyly.

"Skippy, I am going to take him home now but I hear your mother calling you. She sounds worried. You had better run home. I'll see you later this afternoon and we'll go and visit Little Ben at his farm.

Lucky Horseshoes   16

That afternoon Skippy and Iris walked over to the farm. As they got near, Little Ben recognized Skippy and let out a loud whinny and ran over to greet her. His little tail was wagging back and forth and he tried to get Skippy to chase him around the paddock. Just then Annabel, the owner of the farm saw them and came over to greet Skippy.

Annabel explained that Little Ben's legs were unsteady because he had been born a few weeks early, but she hoped that with help and exercise he would get stronger. As Iris and Skippy were leaving, Annabel invited Skippy to come and visit Little Ben whenever she wanted.

"I'll come often," Skippy answered, as she gave Little Ben one final hug.

  Lucky Horseshoes

Winter

Almost every day after school, Skippy visited Little Ben. Even when it was cold outside, the stable was cozy and warm. Iris would keep Skippy and Little Ben amused with her many stories of magical dragons that could fly all over the world.

One afternoon, Skippy was late. Iris was in the barn, sitting on a bale of straw, waiting for her.

"What's the problem?" she asked, as Skippy raced in, out of breath.

"Oh, Iris I got into trouble again at school. I'm not supposed to leave my seat. But sometimes it's hard for me to sit still and I need to move. I can't seem to concentrate on my work. My teacher made me stay after school to catch up on my math. I wish I didn't ever have to go to school. I can't seem to do anything right there."

"Don't worry, Skippy. Just think of what a good job you do here at the stables," Iris replied.

"But that's easy. I really like being here." Skippy said. "I wish I could stay here all the time."

"Well, perhaps you could come here more often. Annabel needs help in the barn and maybe you could do some work for her, suggested Iris."

"That's a great idea, Skippy answered excitedly. Just wait here Iris, and I'll go ask her."

In a few minutes, Skippy ran back beaming.

"Annabel said that if my mom agrees, I could come three times a week and on Saturday's to help clean the stalls and work with Little Ben. His legs are still weak and he needs exercise. Annabel said I could help him get big and strong so he might be a famous jumping horse just like his father. Oh Iris, I'm so happy."

When Skippy's mother heard about this plan, she thought it was a great idea. Helping at the barn would keep Skippy busy and make her feel better about herself.

Skippy loved her new job. Cleaning out the stables was hard work, but when her chores were done, she could spend all her time with Little Ben. She brushed his coat until it shone. To make his legs stronger, she exercised him by slowly leading him around and around on a halter and lead rope.

One day, a terrible thing happened at school. Skippy's teacher had asked her to clean out the rabbit cages. Skippy was sure she could do a good job. If she could clean out a horse stall, she could clean a cage. But just as Skippy was finishing, she thought of something she wanted to do with Little Ben and ran off forgetting to lock the rabbit cages.

The next day, when she arrived at school, the rabbits were hopping around the classroom and down the halls. The other kids thought this was hilarious, but the teacher scolded Skippy for not locking the cage doors.

Skippy's mother was worried. "Skippy, if you are so forgetful, you might forget to lock the stable door and the horses could get out."

Skippy was furious. "You can't stop me from seeing Little Ben. He really needs me and I'm helping him get better. It's not fair. My friend Iris the Dragon says I'm doing a wonderful job. So does Annabel," she cried as she raced out the door.

Lucky Horseshoes

With tears of anger streaming down her face, Skippy ran to the stables. No one was around so she opened the door to Little Ben's stall and curled up in the hay. The colt put his nose down and gently nuzzled her. He lay down beside her to keep her warm and soon they were both sound asleep.

Skippy was wakened from a deep dream by voices calling to each other.

"Here she is," someone cried, peering over the stall door.

As she looked up, Skippy saw strange faces looking down at her. In the crowd she saw her mom, looking very upset.

Skippy thought her mom would be really mad that she had run away. But as they walked home along the river path, Skippy's mother said to her, "Skippy I know you didn't mean to do anything wrong. But we didn't know where you were."

"Sorry, Mom," Skippy replied. "I got so angry I just ran and ran and then I fell asleep in Little Ben's stall."

"I have a suggestion," her mother answered. "Both you and Little Ben have a condition. He has weak muscles in his legs and needs special help. You may have a chemical imbalance in your brain, and you too might need special help. If you and Little Ben both work hard, I know things will get a lot better for you both. He may even get strong enough that you can show him at the summer fair. What do you think?"

"I really want things to get better at school and I really want to help Little Ben," Skippy answered. "Let me think it over Mom."

The next day, Iris was waiting for Skippy down at the riverbank. When Skippy told her what had happened, Iris said, "Little Ben may never be a jumper like his father, but with care and exercise he might one day run without a limp. You want that for him, don't you Skippy?"

"Oh yes, with all my heart," answered Skippy.

"Well, your mother wants to do the same for you. She hopes that with treatment and care you will be able to do better at school. Will you let your mom and the teachers help you, and we will both help Little Ben?" Iris asked while reaching into her knapsack.

Pulling out an old horseshoe from her pack, Iris said, "and to help you both achieve your dreams, I think we should put this horseshoe over Little Ben's stall door. I know it will bring you and Little Ben good luck."

Spring

The weeks passed quickly. The days got warmer and the snow was melting. One afternoon, Skippy heard a sound high in the sky. Looking up, she saw a flock of Canadian geese flying north, and she knew spring had come.

As Skippy was leading Little Ben around the outdoor paddock on a warm April morning, Annabel came up smiling.

"Now that Little Ben can exercise outside, I think we should get to work on a special program for him," she said. "The vet came yesterday and gave Little Ben a full checkup. He said we should give him new feed and extra vitamins. Also, Barry the ferrier is coming tomorrow to work on Little Ben's hooves which will help his legs. I will show you how to halter train Little Ben for the shows. If all goes well, you may be able to show him at the local fair this summer."

Skippy's mom was also arranging a program for Skippy. First, Skippy went with her to visit her doctor. She gave her a full medical checkup and suggested that Skippy and her mother consult with other doctors who were specialists in mental health in order to understand Skippy's illness.

Next, her mother had a long meeting with the school principal and they agreed that it would benefit Skippy if she had a set of tests called psycho-educational assessments.

What's that Mom?" asked Skippy, sounding worried.

"They are tests to figure out how we can find ways to help you do better in school. Just like the vet checked out Little Ben and suggested how he could get stronger, experts will test you and recommend how you can do better in school and be more relaxed," replied Skippy's Mom.

Skippy was a little worried about these tests, but she knew they would help. She was very patient and tried her best to cooperate. She thought of what Little Ben had to go through with the Vet and how brave he was. Skippy couldn't disappoint Little Ben.

A few weeks later when Skippy saw Iris, she told her about what had happened.

"Iris, I have my own IEP," Skippy said proudly.

"That's wonderful and what is your IEP?" asked Iris.

"Well, my tests showed that I have attention deficit disorder with hyperactivity and that I need extra help to do well in school. My principal gave me my own educational program which means my teacher can help me in different ways. At first I was scared that the other kids would tease me, but they don't. I really like my new program. I understand things better and I got a really good report card last week.

Also, my mom has created a special reward program for me to keep me focused and on task. And when I get upset and angry at my mom, I am sent to my room for a quiet time. I don't run away anymore and my room is a safe place to calm down."

"I'm so proud of you," said Iris. "You have your own IEP and Little Ben has his own IEEP."

"What do you mean?" asked Skippy looking puzzled.

"His very own Individual Exercise and Eating Plan," Iris replied, laughing. "You're in charge of the exercise and I'll help with the food. I'm going right home to check my magic recipe books so that I can prepare special foods to help Little Ben grow stronger. Bye Skippy."

Summer

Skippy was bursting with excitement. It was the last day of school and the opening of the county fair was in two days. Skippy had spent many months exercising Little Ben and Annabel felt he was now strong enough to show.

School ended with a party for the students, their parents and the teachers. The principal gave a short speech and presented awards to the most outstanding students.

Then the principal stepped up to the podium again and said, "today we have a new award to give - a prize for the student who has made the most progress. And the winner of that prize is Skippy."

Everyone burst into applause. Skippy was so happy she felt like crying. She gave her mom a big hug and said, "thank you Mom for all your help."

As Skippy was leaving, she saw Iris sitting quietly under the apple tree near the playground. Skippy ran over to see her.

"Oh, Iris," she cried. "I am so happy today. I won the prize for the student who made the most progress. It's a book about horses. I used to really hate school. It made me feel so anxious. But now that I understand what they are teaching me, I get my work done and I really like it."

"I knew you would do well, Skippy. A lot of people worked hard to help you. But you worked the hardest. We are all very proud of you," Iris answered. "I have a gift for you too. You'll see it when you go to the stable tomorrow."

"Oh, Iris. Please tell me what is it?" Skippy laughed, hopping up and down and pulling at Iris's knapsack.

"Wait and see," called Iris as she jumped into the river and swam upstream.

Bright and early the next morning, Skippy arrived at the stables. She had a lot to do today. She wanted to make sure that Little Ben was ready for the fair tomorrow. She was also curious to see what Iris had given her.

As she opened the stall door, Little Ben gave a knicker and trotted up to show Skippy his new red halter.

"Oh, Little Ben, you look beautiful," cried Skippy, giving Little Ben a big hug.

Just at that moment, Iris appeared at the stable door.

"Iris, I love it," cried Skippy, hugging Iris hard around her neck. "Even if Little Ben doesn't win a prize, he'll be the best looking horse at the show."

Iris and Skippy spent the day brushing Little Ben until his coat shone. When Skippy agreed they had done all they could do, Iris reached up into her hat and took out three tiny silver horseshoes.

"Tie these into Little Ben's mane for good luck," she said as she handed them to Skippy.

Skippy put the little horseshoes into Little Ben's mane, stepped back and said, "you are beautiful Little Ben and I think we are ready for tomorrow."

"Goodnight Iris," said Skippy. "You're a very special friend. You're always there when I need you."

"And you're a very special person Skippy. I know Little Ben and you have worked hard this year to achieve your dreams."

  Lucky Horseshoes

The next day at the summer fair, Skippy led Little Ben into the show ring. She felt relaxed and happy and looked forward to the day's events.

She knew that Little Ben looked handsome. She felt sure he would do his very best. Everyone watched as she put him through his paces. He lifted his legs high and trotted proudly around the ring with Skippy. Then he stood very still while they waited for the judge's decision.

As the judge came towards the horses, Skippy took a deep breath. The judge paused for a few seconds giving all the horses one final look. Then he walked towards Little Ben and Skippy. He smiled and hung the red ribbon on Little Ben's halter.

"Congratulations," he said as the crowd cheered.

Skippy threw her arms around Little Ben's neck and yelled,

"We did it, Little Ben. We did it."

Epilogue to: "Lucky Horseshoes —
A Tale from the Iris the Dragon Series"

Dr. Catharine Robertson
Staff Psychiatrist, Children's Hospital of Eastern Ontario
Chair, ADHD Network of Eastern Ontario

If Skippy were a real child, she may well have the combined type of ADHD (Attention-Deficit/Hyperactivity Disorder). This means, compared to other children her age, she may be significantly more inattentive (have difficulty "focusing", or being too easily "distracted" or "daydreaming"), as well as hyperactive (overly active, "restless", "fidgety" or unable to stay seated), and/or impulsive (doing or saying things as soon as they come into her mind without first thinking of the possible consequences). ADHD is a common problem in school-aged children such that there is usually at least one child in each community-based class with ADHD.

Many children have some difficulties concentrating or sitting still at some time in their lives. Many have found themselves regretting having said or done something without thinking. These children would not be diagnosed as having ADHD unless it was causing them impairment such as not achieving in school to their potential or not being able to have harmonious relationships in the home and/or with others their age. They must also have a certain number of the symptoms of ADHD in order to be diagnosed with it. These symptoms must be seen in more than one setting. Most children with ADHD have inherited these difficulties, which can be seen early in life and don't just start suddenly later in school (although children can become more obviously less able to cope as the demands for independent study increase). Many children with ADHD will go into adulthood with ADHD symptoms.

The way in which ADHD is diagnosed may be unexpected. There is no blood test for ADHD. It is diagnosed by looking at difficulties experienced by the child and those around the child. Information is obtained from the child, family, and teachers (or others) verbally and is often complemented by questionnaires. Parents are asked whether difficulties run in the family. Psychologists are often asked to perform psycho educational assessments on the child. In order for ADHD to be diagnosed, the symptoms cannot be better explained by physical or other mental health or educational issues. Prescription medications cannot cure ADHD but can help control its symptoms. Educating the family and child about ADHD, behavior management (techniques aimed at encouraging wanted behaviour and decreasing unwanted behaviour), educational programming and strategies, and where needed, individual and family counseling, are often part of treatment packages. The treatment of co-occurring health issues is often also involved.

Although it is still thought that ADHD is seen more often in boys than girls, Skippy does show some signs of ADHD. Her name is a clue to her disorder in that she has a hard time sitting still and is always skipping about (hyperactivity). She tends to get into trouble for daydreaming or being distracted and not getting done what is she is told to do, be it schoolwork or tasks such as locking up the rabbit cage (inattention). We get a glimpse of her impulsivity when she does things without thinking and later regrets what she has done. We can also see how, because she has the feeling she "just can't do things right" that, although this currently makes her irritable, it may eventually lower her self esteem and/or lead to problems with depression or anxiety.

Fortunately for Skippy, her mother spoke not only with the school but also with the family doctor, which led to a full assessment of Skippy. Sometimes family physicians feel comfortable making the diagnosis of ADHD themselves but sometimes they prefer to consult with (seek the advice of) psychologists or medical doctors such as psychiatrists, pediatricians, and some other medical specialists, all of whom may make the diagnosis. Only medical doctors can prescribe medications. Skippy had a psycho educational assessment, which would have involved testing done by a psychologist to see what she is capable of intellectually and comparing this with how she is achieving academically. Certain patterns, which tend to be seen on testing children with ADHD, can sometimes be seen and commented on by the psychologist. Psychologists also use psycho educational testing to help decide whether a child has a learning disability instead of, or in addition to, ADHD.

It was not mentioned in the story as to whether Skippy was prescribed medications but if she had it would likely have been a stimulant (e.g. methylphenidate as in Ritalin, Focalin, Metadate, or Concerta, or an amphetamine as in Dexedrine, Dexedrine Spansules, Adderall, or Adderrall XR) or an antidepressant such as atomoxetine (as in Strattera). These stimulants and atomoxetine are approved by both Health Canada and the FDA and for the front line treatment of ADHD. Although other medications are sometimes used especially if a child has a combination of ADHD and another difficulty. As new studies are done, medications used in ADHD may change with time so please ask your doctor about this.

Skippy was, however, discussed by a committee at school which would have had input from those who were working with Skippy at school and from those who had assessed or tested Skippy. The committee would have been able to identify Skippy's strengths and weaknesses and would have ensured she received the help at school she needed. Skippy was given an IEP (Individual Education Plan), which would have taken her strengths and weaknesses into account.

Skippy was lucky in that she was diagnosed with, and was treated for, ADHD by professionals. She also received help from Iris and Annabel in that they were able to get Skippy involved in helping Little Ben, an activity at which Skippy was both capable and motivated. Skippy's pride in this might well have boosted her self-esteem.

It sounds as if Skippy's mother attended a parent group for parents of children with ADHD. Not only would this have helped Skippy's mother understand more about ADHD and what to do about it but it would have provided her with support. ADHD children may be more of a challenge to parents. Parent groups are helpful for parents to learn they are not alone in this and that others can understand. It is also useful to learn from each other's experiences in addition to what is taught (about ADHD and about behaviour management) by the group leader.

By the end of the story it is clear through Skippy's award that her schoolwork had improved. She also seemed to be doing well socially. Others are not as fortunate as Skippy in that ADHD many go undiagnosed and/or untreated. The burden these children have to carry through life is no less important than other disabilities be they physical or otherwise. Proper diagnosis and treatment can make a lot of difference in the lives of these children.

If you would like more information on ADHD, a good place to start is with reputable national organizations for ADHD such as CHADD (Children and Adults with Attention-Deficit/Hyperactivity Disorder) or ADDA (Attention Deficit Disorder Association). Medical Associations such as the AAP (American Academy of Pediatrics), and the AACAP (American Academy of Child and Adolescent Psychiatry), provide information about ADHD on their websites. The CACAP (Canadian Academy of Child and Adolescent Psychiatry) joins the AAP and the AACAP in producing medical journals, which include articles on ADHD. CADDRA (Canadian ADHD Resource Alliance) has a website with information from (and for) physicians. Research institutions such as the NIH (National Institute of Health) with its NIMH (National Institute of Mental Health) can provide information and have their own websites. The above provide information reviewed by doctors and/or scientists. Some of the above websites will recommend books, but general booklists can be found by searching under ADHD on the website of your favourite bookstore chain (e.g. www.chapters.indigo.ca or www.bn.com) or specialty book warehouses (e.g. www.addwarehouse.com). These books may or may not reflect recognized opinion.

Web Sites (in the order in which they were mentioned above):

www.chadd.org   www.health.nih.gov
www.nimh.nih.gov   www.caddra.ca
www.add.org
www.aap.org
www.aacap.org

Educator's Page

Educators play an important role in identifying and helping children with mental illness. With the increase of stress and stimulation in our fast paced world, mental health problems in children are becoming more prevalent and the result is falling heavily on educators.

Iris the Dragon Inc. has developed tools to help educators address mental health issues in the classroom. Available from Iris the Dragon Inc. are a 'Teacher's Workbook: A Guide to Understanding Mental Illness in the Classroom,' lesson plans, school awareness programs and more. Below is a brief explanation of the tools.

Iris the Dragon's teacher workbook is a guide to help teachers understand mental illness in children and provide resources to help assist these children in the classroom.

The workbook includes:
- the definition of mental illness,
- the causes of mental illness,
- identifying early warning signs,
- what to do with a child who is suffering from mental health symptoms (Ontario specific school guidelines), and
- ideas on how to cope with mental health problems in the classroom
- including the Iris the Dragon puppet show kit – 'Summer Magic'

The 'Summer Magic' puppet kit provides educators the opportunity to have children become more involved in a dialogue about mental health. Through creating the puppets and performing a skit, students begin to identify with the characters in 'Summer Magic' and understand the challenges people face when involved with a mental health issue.

Iris the Dragon Inc. lesson plans and awareness programs are available for download on our website. The lesson plans and programs provide activities to use with the Iris the Dragon Book Series to draw out a dialogue and understanding of mental health issues.

For more information on our Educator's tools, please visit www.iristhedragon.com, Educator's Page.

Author: Gayle Grass

Gayle Grass is an author of children's books and the mother of a child who suffers from a mental illness. Her decision to write illustrated children's books came from the sincere belief that his medium could be used to break down the stigma and fears surrounding mental illness and encourage a dialogue between children and their caregivers. Children need a language to express their feelings and Iris the Dragon teaches it to them through her gentle understanding manner. Gayle obtained her masters degree at the University of London England in Art History. She did her thesis on "Private Presses and the Art of Book Making". Books provide a wonderful medium to stimulate many of our senses; sight, hearing, smell and touch. Children who suffer from a mental illness have a distortion of their senses and therefore view their world from a different perspective. Illustrated books provide an alternative medium to communicate to children with mental health disorders. Gayle believes reading books to children with mental illness will help them understand that there are solutions and they are not alone.

Illustrator: Linda Crockett

Winner of many National and International awards, Linda has achieved recognition as an illustrator. Her work is included in the Society of Illustrators permanent Collection featuring her 2 Gold Medals at their 24th Annual Exhibition. Linda's work as an outstanding illustrator was rewarded by her Alumni Association and she received the Distinguished Achievement Hall of Frame Award, the Euclid Community Enrichment Award and an Ohio State Senate Commendation for Art Achievement. Her children's book illustrations have been honored at the Euclid Children's' Book Fair and she received the Cleveland Press Club Award for Excellence in illustration. Linda resides in Euclid, Ohio.

How to get in touch with Iris:

Please write to:

Iris the Dragon Inc.
Grassmere Farms
1545 Rideau Ferry Rd.
Perth, ON
Canada
K7H 3C7

Phone:

Tel: 613-267-5601
Fax: 613-267-6693

Email: info@iristhedragon.com

Web site: www.iristhedragon.com

Sponsorships

Iris the Dragon Inc. is enormously grateful for the support of the following organizations and individuals without whose help and encouragement this book could never have been completed.

F.K. Morrow Foundation

Special thanks to the CHEO Foundation (Children's Hospital of Eastern Ontario) for their continued support of this project and assistance in establishing the Iris the Dragon Fund to help children with mental health issues.